THE PUPPY PLACE

LOUIE

THE PUPPY PLACE

Don't miss any of these other stories by Ellen Miles!

THE PUPPY PLACE

LOUIE

WITHDRAWN

ELLEN MILES

SCHOLASTIC INC.

Copyright © 2018 by Ellen Miles
Cover art by Tim O'Brien
Original cover design by Steve Scott

ISBN 978-1-338-21267-9

10 9 8 7 6 5 4 3   18 19 20 21 22

Printed in the U.S.A.   40
First printing 2018

For all my friends who love big dogs!

CHAPTER ONE

"Over here!" Charles Peterson called to his best friend, Sammy. "I need your help with this one." He grabbed one end of a huge dead branch—more like a tree, practically!—and tugged as hard as he could. It didn't move.

Sammy trotted over. "That's a big one," he said, looking down at the branch. "Let's drag it over to the fire pit. It'll make awesome firewood for the party later on."

It was a chilly day in May. A few patches of blue polka-dotted the mostly gray sky. Charles and Sammy, and the rest of their Cub Scout den, were busy helping to clean up Loon Lake Park for the summer season. When they were done, their families would meet them there and they would celebrate with the first cookout of the year.

Charles and Sammy were on the "pick-up" team. Their job was to pick up any branches or twigs that had fallen during the winter. Other teams were gathering trash and raking leaves.

They were working hard, but Charles didn't mind. It was fun to be at the park before the official opening day. In a few weeks, there would be kids racing around the playground, and noisy volleyball games, and swimmers and kayakers splashing in the water. Now, everything was quiet and peaceful. The grass was just starting to turn green, the leaves on the trees were tender and new, and the colorful canoes and kayaks were still stacked on shore, waiting for their first voyages across the lake.

Springtime at Loon Lake Park was special, but

Charles also liked being there in the middle of winter, when his family had a tradition of having a picnic each year. It was even quieter when the park was closed for the season and they had to hike in. Everything looked so different when snow covered the grassy areas and thick ice trapped the sparkling waters of the lake.

Charles would never forget the winter day when his family had seen a puppy fall through the ice. That had been so scary, but with the help of a special cold-water rescue team, they had saved the curly-haired pup. Noodle had become one of the Petersons' favorite foster puppies as they tried to find out where he belonged. Lizzie, Charles's older sister, got especially attached to Noodle and had a hard time saying good-bye to him when the time came. But that was what fostering was all about: the Petersons only kept each puppy long enough to find him or her the perfect forever home. Even the Bean, Charles's younger brother, understood that.

"Remember Noodle?" Charles asked Sammy now as they dragged the big branch toward the fire pit, a ring of stones near the sandy beach. It was slow going, but with both of them pulling hard, they could keep moving.

"Of course," said Sammy. "I remember every single one of your foster puppies."

Sammy and his parents lived right next door to the Petersons, so he had met all the dogs who had stayed with Charles's family. Sammy and his family had even adopted one of them: Goldie the golden retriever, the very first puppy the Petersons had ever fostered.

"Ready? One, two, three," chanted Charles as he and Sammy heaved their big branch into the fire pit. They stood back and brushed off their hands, breathing hard.

"Nice work, boys," said Charles's dad. "We're going to have a huge bonfire tonight. I hope we have enough marshmallows!"

Charles grinned up at him. He was glad that his parents were Akelas—leaders—of his Cub Scout den. It made everything the den did even more fun. Mom was home working on a story for the local newspaper, but she had promised to come down to the park with Lizzie and the Bean when she was done. Charles's dad was on call for his job as a firefighter, but unless his pager went off, he wouldn't have to leave. Some of the other scouts' parents were there, just in case.

"Are we having hot dogs, too?" Sammy asked. Sammy was always hungry, always thinking about food.

"You bet," said Charles's dad. "And I think your mom said she was bringing over some of her famous potato salad."

Charles's stomach grumbled. "I'm already hungry," he said.

"We're almost done," said Dad. "See how the grass looks even greener than it did when we got here? All that raking really pays off. And you boys have done an excellent job picking up most of the sticks. Everything is looking terrific." He bent to rummage in his backpack. "Here, have a snack and then we can finish up." He handed Charles and Sammy a cheese stick each and some crackers.

After they'd eaten, the boys headed off, scanning the grass for the last of the sticks and branches. "Hey," said Charles. "Check it out." He leaned over to pick up an old tennis ball. After a winter under the snow, it was more gray than green, and one side was a little bald. "It's kind of ratty, but Buddy will love it. I'll take it home for him."

Buddy was the Petersons' little brown puppy,

the best puppy in the universe. He had come to them as a foster puppy, but the whole family had fallen in love with him, and they had decided that Buddy's perfect home was right there, with them. Now he slept on Charles's bed almost every night (when Lizzie didn't steal him), and waited eagerly for Charles every day after school. He was the cutest, sweetest, most fun puppy Charles had ever known, and he got along great with all the Petersons' foster puppies.

Charles shoved the ball into his jacket pocket and went back to hunting for more sticks. There weren't many. The park was looking really tidy after all their work, and Charles could just picture himself one day soon, running barefoot in the grass in his bathing suit. The sun would be warm on his back, but if he got too hot, all he'd have to do was run down to the dock and leap off into the cool, clear, refreshing—

"Charles!"

He heard his dad shouting, and turned to see his father waving at him from across the grass. Charles ran back to the fire pit. "What is it? Did you get paged? Do you have to go?"

Dad shook his head. He was holding his phone in one hand. "Mom just called. She saw an alert online. Somebody reported that there's an abandoned puppy who needs help."

"What?" Charles asked. "Where?"

"Right here," said Dad. "Right here at Loon Lake Park."

CHAPTER TWO

Charles stared at his dad. "Here, in the park?" he asked. Even though he had heard Dad perfectly well, he couldn't believe his ears.

Dad nodded. "A runner just reported an abandoned puppy in the upper parking lot. She posted it on this special page for lost and missing dogs." He was already walking quickly toward the trail that led to the upper parking area. Charles trotted after him, and Sammy followed along.

"What's going on?" called Hunter Pagano, one of the other scouts. He and his twin brother, Tyler, were in the other second-grade class at Charles's school, Littleton Elementary. Sammy and the other scout in their den, Liam Poole, were in Mr. Mason's class, with Charles.

"There's a puppy we have to help," called Charles.

The twins threw down their rakes and ran over. Their mom followed behind. "A puppy?" she asked Charles's dad when they caught up.

"That's what I hear," he said. "Let's go find out."

By the time they reached the trail, Liam had joined them as well, leaving the tarp he'd been using to drag raked-up leaves.

"I love dogs," said Hunter as the group crossed the little footbridge and climbed the big wooden stairs that led to the parking lot. "We used to have one named Sadie. She was too wild so we had to find her a new home, but I liked her."

"She liked me better," said Tyler. "She always slept on my bed."

"Not always," said Hunter.

"Usually," said Tyler.

"Boys," said Mrs. Pagano, shaking her head. "How do you make everything into an argument? Sadie loved both of you, but neither of you is really old enough to remember her much."

"I remember her," said Tyler. "She was black and white and she was really soft, especially her ears."

"I remember her better," said Hunter. "She liked to lick my face."

Hunter and Tyler's mom stepped between them on the trail. "That's enough," she said.

"I have a dog," said Liam. "Well, he's not really my dog—he's my grammy's. But I get to play with him all the time. His name is Buster."

Up front, Charles's dad nodded. "We all love dogs, don't we?" By then they were at the top of the trail. Charles looked up one side of the big parking lot and down the other. In summer, the parking lot would be full of cars roasting in the sun, but now it was empty. Except—what was that? "There!" He pointed. "Do you think the puppy is in that crate?"

At the far end of the parking lot was a large white plastic box, the type that people used when they were traveling with a dog. It had a small window on the side, but from this distance Charles couldn't see if anything was in there.

The whole group broke into a trot, with Charles leading the way across the parking lot. As he grew nearer, he began to hear a high-pitched whimpering. He sped up, running as fast as he could. Poor puppy! Who would leave a little dog locked up all alone like that?

He was the first to arrive at the box. Now he could see something through the wire-mesh window. White fur—maybe some black fur, too? A pink tongue, panting. A shiny black eye staring back at him.

"It is a puppy—it really is," Charles called as he reached for the latch.

"Wait, Charles!" Dad caught up and touched Charles's shoulder. "We don't know anything about this dog. Let's take it slow. We can't just let him out."

"But Dad," Charles said, "listen to him."

The whimpering was louder now, punctuated by small yips and barks. The puppy banged around inside the cage as if he was fighting to get out. Charles pictured a wiry little terrier, bouncing around like a jumping bean.

"Okay, okay," Dad said soothingly. "Don't worry, fella. We're here to help." He looked around at the circle of boys who had crowded around the crate. "Everybody stand back, all right?"

Hunter took one step back, but came closer again when he noticed that Tyler hadn't moved. Everyone else stood where they were, staring at the crate. "I'm sure it's safe," said Hunter and Tyler's mom. "It's just a little puppy, right?"

Dad shrugged and knelt down to open the door of the crate. "Oof!" he said as something big and furry erupted out of the box, knocking him over.

"Whoa!" said Charles as he jumped forward to grab the dog. "That is one giant puppy!"

Hunter and Tyler piled on, Hunter by the dog's head and Tyler by his tail. Sammy stood in front of the dog, hands out to block the pup from running past him. Liam threw his arms around the puppy's neck.

The puppy squirmed and wriggled, but he couldn't get away. Charles felt for a collar, but all he found was thick, curly fur. "Dad," he said. "How are we going to hold him?"

By now, Dad was back on his feet. "Let's all calm down," he said. "Everybody off the dog. I don't think he'll go anywhere."

Sure enough, when all the boys had let go, the puppy shook himself off. His shaggy coat was white, with big splotches of black. He had big ears that hung down, a massive head, giant paws, a big wet pink tongue, and a big white fluffy tail. He gazed around at all the people. Then he turned and ran right back into the crate.

CHAPTER THREE

"Hey, wait," said Charles. "Hey, pup, did we scare you?"

Tyler bent down to look into the crate. "Come on out of there," he said. "Come on, puppy!" He reached in as if to grab the big shaggy pup.

"Don't!" said Charles. "He's afraid. Too many people—or something. Whatever it is, we scared him." Tyler's mom pulled him away, and Charles pushed the crate's door shut so the puppy would feel safe.

"How could we scare anyone?" asked Hunter. "We're just a bunch of kids."

"Some dogs just aren't used to a lot of people or activity at once," said Charles.

Dad nodded. "And we can't know what happened to him before he was abandoned here."

Liam's eyes widened. "Like—maybe somebody was mean to him?" he asked.

"We just don't know," said Dad.

"For that matter, we don't know if he might be mean himself," said Mrs. Pagano. "I think we should give this pup some space. Tyler, Hunter, come help me get our picnic food out of the car."

"But—" Tyler began.

"No buts," said his mom. "Charles and his dad know much more about dogs than we do. Let's let them figure out what to do next. Liam and Sammy, you come along, too. I bet your parents will be arriving any minute." She marched the boys off toward the lower parking lot. Hunter looked back over his shoulder, but his mom kept him moving.

Charles and Dad looked at each other. "So, what do we do?" Charles asked.

Dad smiled. "We wait. I think now that things are a little calmer, he'll be ready to come back out very soon."

Charles sat down cross-legged on the ground. He found a spot near the crate, but not right in front of it. He could see the puppy watching him through the wire mesh. His big furry head filled nearly the whole window, and he had to hunch over to fit inside the crate now that he was sitting up. "It's okay, puppy," Charles said. "Nobody's going to grab you."

Dad sat down, too. "Poor guy," he said. "What was somebody thinking, to leave him here all on his own? He may be big, but he's still just a youngster." He shook his head.

The puppy pushed his nose toward the wire mesh and sniffed. "Dad, look," Charles said in a low voice. "I think he's kind of interested in us."

"Mmm hmmm," agreed Dad. "Put your hand out — slowly, now!"

Charles reached his hand toward the crate. The puppy shrank back. "It's okay," Charles said in his quietest voice. "It's okay, Louie."

"Louie?" Dad asked, also quietly. "How do you know his name?"

"I don't," said Charles. "He just seems like a Louie."

Dad smiled. "Louie seems to like that name," he said, nodding at the crate.

The puppy had his nose stuck up against the mesh again. Charles moved his hand just a little bit closer so he was touching the other side of the wire window. He felt the dog's warm breath on his fingers as the puppy snuffled and sniffed.

"That's right," Charles said in a whisper. "See? I'm okay."

"Sit right there," said Dad. "I'm going to open the door to his crate again. This time when he comes out, you won't grab him, right?"

"Of course I won't," said Charles. He felt bad that he'd scared the pup the first time around. "I just didn't want him to run away."

"I think he'll stay around," Dad said. "I have a feeling he likes you."

Charles smiled. He had that feeling, too. He had kept his hand at the window, and the puppy was nuzzling his fingers with his soft nose through the wire mesh.

"Okay, here goes," said Dad. Slowly, he reached over to open the door to the crate.

Charles held his breath. The puppy turned his head toward the front of the crate to see what was happening. Carefully, Charles shifted just a little bit so the puppy could see him through the door. "Come on, Louie," he whispered. "Come on out and say hi."

The pup put one big paw out of the crate, then another. He craned his neck to look at Charles, tilting his head.

Is it safe? I'd like to get to know you better, but I'm scared.

"It's okay, big boy," Charles said softly. "Come on." He made a little kissing noise with his mouth. "Come on, pup."

The puppy eased his way out of the crate, glancing first at Dad—who sat still as a statue—then at Charles. Two big paws, a big head, and then the rest of him emerged from the crate. Once out, he shook himself again. Then he padded over to Charles and lay down next to him, putting a paw in Charles's lap.

"Oh!" said Charles. "What a good boy. Good boy, Louie." Gently, he gave the pup a scratch between the ears. The dog's big fluffy tail thumped on the ground as he gazed up at Charles.

Dad smiled. "He trusts you," he said.

Charles grinned back at him. "I think we might have just met our newest foster puppy," he said.

"Uh—hold on there, chief," said Dad. "I'm not so sure about that."

CHAPTER FOUR

Charles stared at his father. "What do you mean?"

"Well," said Dad, "he's an awfully big puppy, and fostering him could be an awfully big job. Remember Boomer?"

Charles grinned. How could he forget the giant, slobbery puppy the Petersons had once fostered? Boomer had been sweet, but maybe a little— clumsy. And he shed. A lot. "Yeah, so? That turned out okay in the end."

"Maybe," Dad said. "If you don't count a few broken vases, some ruined clothes, and a giant food bill."

"We've fostered little dogs that were more

trouble," Charles reminded him. He stroked Louie's big head, which now lay heavily in Charles's lap. Louie seemed to feel very comfortable with Charles already. "What about Daisy?"

Dad laughed. "True. That pup was pretty destructive. Our couch has never been the same." He held up his hands. "We'll talk it over as a family. Speaking of which, I bet your mom and the others are here by now, getting our picnic ready. Let's see if our furry friend is ready to join the party."

"What do you think, Louie?" Charles put his arms around the big pup's neck. "I promise you'll be safe."

The black-and-white pup nuzzled Charles's ear until Charles giggled. Then he thumped his big tail on the ground again.

Whatever you say. I trust you now.

"I guess we'll just have to hope that he'll stay with us until we find a leash and collar for him," said Dad.

"I think he'll want to stick around once he finds out that we're having hot dogs," Charles said. He stood up, only to find out that his foot was asleep from sitting cross-legged for so long with a big dog head on his lap. He stood on one foot and circled the other until he felt the pins and needles that meant it was coming back to life. "Come on, Louie. Let's go get you a treat."

The puppy seemed to know that word. He looked up eagerly and nuzzled Charles's pocket, wagging his tail.

Treats? I'm totally into treats.

Charles laughed. "I don't have any yet. But we'll find you something as soon as we can." He petted the puppy's big long ears. "Good boy," he said as they began to walk back toward the lake.

They walked quietly for a while. Then Charles spoke up. "Dad? How could anybody abandon such a great dog?"

Dad shook his head. "They probably thought they had a good reason. But there's never a good reason to leave a dog like that. If they couldn't keep him, they should have brought him to Caring Paws."

Charles nodded. "And then Ms. Dobbins probably would have called us to foster him, anyway," he said with a grin. Ms. Dobbins was the director of the local animal shelter. Charles's older sister, Lizzie, volunteered there every Saturday, and Charles often helped out, too. For his next birthday, he was planning to ask everyone to donate food and supplies to Caring Paws.

"You're probably right about that," Dad

admitted. "But still, it has to be a family decision to take on a foster pup of this size. Let's see what your mom thinks."

Charles wanted to run on ahead and find Mom and ask her—beg her!—to let him foster Louie. He was already crazy about this big dude with the big black spots and the huge, feathery tail.

"Maybe you should run on ahead and—"

Charles looked at his dad. How did he do that? It was like he was reading Charles's mind.

"—tell the other kids to take it easy when the puppy gets there," Dad finished.

"Oh, right," said Charles. "Good idea." He saw that they were about to come out at the bottom of the trail, by the lake. "Can you hold Louie?"

Dad knelt down and put his arms around the big pup. "Ha, ha, cut it out!" he said when the puppy licked his face.

"See? He likes you, too," said Charles.

"Go on," said Dad, smiling.

Charles ran down the path toward the cluster of people near one of the picnic tables on the lakeshore. As he got closer, he saw that Mom was there with Lizzie and the Bean, and Liam's parents, and Sammy's dad. The twins' father had arrived, too. The adults were setting food out on the picnic table while the boys kicked a soccer ball around.

"Hey, everybody," Charles called. "Hey, we got the puppy to come back out. He's on his way here." He paused, panting. "But he's kind of shy, so everybody has to be calm. Okay?"

The twins' dad laughed. "I hear he's kind of a wimp," he said.

Charles stopped in his tracks and frowned. He didn't like that. "No, he isn't," he said. "Louie's just not used to lots of people jumping on him."

Mom put her hands on his shoulders. "We

understand, Charles. We'll be careful not to scare him. Right, boys?"

"Right," chorused Sammy, Liam, and Hunter.

But Tyler put his hands on his hips. "Louie?" he said. "How did you find out his name?"

"I just guessed it," said Charles. "He just seems like a Louie."

"I bet I can think of a better name," said Tyler.

Charles shrugged. "Here he comes," he said, pointing to the edge of the woods. Dad and the big black-and-white pup were just emerging from the trail.

CHAPTER FIVE

"A Landseer!" said Lizzie as soon as she spotted the big puppy. "Cool."

"A what?" asked Charles. It was amazing how Lizzie always knew the breed of a puppy or dog the second she saw it.

"It's a type of Newfoundland," Lizzie said. "Instead of being solid black, like most of that breed, Landseers are spotted black and white." She smiled. "It's so perfect that we're at the lake. Newfoundlands are water dogs. They used to rescue fishermen out of the freezing seas off Newfoundland, way up in northern Canada."

"Uppy!" yelled the Bean. Charles grabbed his little brother by the sleeve before he could charge toward the big puppy.

Hunter and Tyler's mom was holding the twins back, too. "Come on, Mom," said Hunter, struggling to get away. "I want to see the puppy."

"You can see him," said his mom. "You just can't jump all over him."

Dad and Louie approached the picnic table. Louie's tail was down, and Charles could see the whites of his eyes as the puppy peered anxiously at the crowd of people. "It's okay," Dad kept telling him. "Nobody's going to hurt you."

Louie hung back, but Dad managed to coax him along until they joined the group. "Okay, easy now, everyone," Dad said. "If you want to say hello to Louie, get down on his level and be very gentle and quiet."

"I brought a leash and collar," said Lizzie, holding them up. "Maybe I should put them on him, to make sure he doesn't run off?"

"Good idea," said Dad.

Lizzie knelt down and spoke softly to Louie as she buckled the collar around his big neck. Then she clipped on the leash. "Good boy," she said. Louie thumped his tail.

"He's so big!" said Liam's mom as the other kids knelt to pet Louie. "This wasn't what I imagined when I reported a dog in a crate."

"You were the runner?" Mom asked Mrs. Poole. "The one who posted the alert about an abandoned dog?"

She nodded. "I didn't know what else to do. I didn't have a leash or a collar or a car. I ran home and put that posting online, then came back here as soon as I could."

"Did you see any vehicles leaving the parking lot?" Mom asked. She pulled a small pad out of her pocket—her reporter's notebook. Charles smiled. His mom knew a good story when she heard one.

Mrs. Poole shook her head. "Not one," she said. "And there was no note on the crate or anything. Poor puppy."

"He'll be fine now," said Lizzie. "Our family will foster him and find him a great home."

Dad cleared his throat. "I'm not so sure about that," he said. "This is a big dog with big needs. Like, a bath for one thing. And some training. We'd want to try to figure out who left him, and find him a great new home—which won't be easy, because of his size. He might just be more than our family is ready for right now."

"I can relate to that," said Hunter and Tyler's

mom. "After our last experience with a dog, I said 'no more dogs, ever.'"

"What happened?" asked Mom. She gestured toward the table. "Why don't we start eating while you tell us? That potato salad is calling my name."

Charles felt his stomach grumble and remembered how hungry he was. Food! What a great idea. He and the other boys gave the puppy a few more pats, then got up to fill their plates along with the adults. Charles made sure to put an extra hot dog on his plate, for Louie.

"So, what happened with your last dog?" Mom asked again as they all sat down to eat.

Mrs. Pagano looked at Mr. Pagano. "I guess we just didn't make the best choice," she said carefully. "Sadie was a big German shepherd–Lab mix."

"Which seemed perfect," said her husband. "A pal for the kids, and a protector for our property."

"But?" asked Mom.

"But she was just a little too wild," said the twins' mom. "She barked nonstop every time someone came to the door, jumped on people, and chased the neighborhood cats."

"And she bit the mailman," said Hunter.

"Right," said his mom. "She bit the mailman. That was kind of the last straw. I have enough on my hands, with these two." She smiled over at the twins. "I can't handle an aggressive dog on top of everything else."

"We took her to a shelter in the town where we used to live. They promised to work with her and find her another home," said Mr. Pagano.

"That must have been a tough decision," said Mrs. Poole, Liam's mom.

"At least you didn't abandon her in a parking lot," said Mom, shaking her head as she gazed down at Louie, who was gobbling a piece of hot dog Charles had just given him. "That is just—just—"

"The worst," said Lizzie. "If I ever find out who did that—"

"We *should* find out," said Hunter, around a mouthful of pasta with pesto. "We can be detectives and follow clues and stuff. Then we can tell those people that what they did was really bad."

Charles looked at him, surprised. "That's a good idea," he said.

"And we could also help get the puppy cleaned up and help train him," said Tyler. "So your family doesn't have to do all the work."

"It can be our next Cub Scout project," said Liam. "It would be great practice for working toward our Animal Care Activity badges."

Charles grinned. "That's a *great* idea!" he said. He turned to his mom and dad. "If it's a den project and we all help a lot, will you say yes to fostering Louie?"

Mom looked at Dad and raised her eyebrows. Dad nodded.

"Yay!" yelled Charles, Lizzie, and the Bean.

CHAPTER SIX

"Hey, cut it out!" yelled Charles. "That water is really cold."

"Oops, sorry," said Hunter. "I was aiming for the puppy."

It was Sunday, the day after the picnic at Loon Lake. Charles had brought Louie over to Tyler and Hunter's house. Sammy came over, too. Now they were giving Louie a bath in the backyard.

At the picnic, the scouts had decided to split into two teams. Hunter and Sammy would get Louie cleaned up, work on his training and socialization, and start trying to find him a new home. Tyler and Liam would try to figure out who had abandoned Louie, and why. Charles was on both teams, since Louie was living at his house.

Louie had settled in well at the Petersons'. He had been shy when he and Buddy first met, but after a few minutes they were best buds. He and Buddy had both slept on Charles's bed, which had not left a whole lot of room for Charles.

Lizzie had done some research on Landseers and had shown Charles a picture of one swimming in the cold Atlantic Ocean. "See?" she said. "These dogs are no wimps."

Meanwhile, Mom had already started writing an article about the puppy who had been abandoned at Loon Lake Park. "My editor said that if I finish it today he can get it in tomorrow's paper," she'd told Charles as she dropped him off at Hunter's. "He thought that a lot of people would be interested in Louie's story."

Now in the Paganos' backyard, Charles looked

at Louie. The big shaggy pup was drenched in water, and Hunter and Sammy were rubbing soap into his fur. He didn't even try to run away, like some dogs did when you gave them a bath. Louie just stood there patiently, head and tail hanging down, waiting for it to be over.

Charles thought Hunter's mom had been right: Louie didn't seem to mind the cold water from the hose. "I guess if he's made for swimming in the northern Atlantic Ocean, a little cold water won't bother him," she'd said. She had agreed to the bath only if the boys did it in the backyard. "Remember, no more dogs for me, ever," she'd said. "Especially big shaggy dogs like this one. Who needs the mess?" But she'd smiled at Louie and petted him when she brought out the bathing supplies: some baby shampoo, a pile of old towels, and a plastic pitcher.

"Good boy, Louie," said Charles as he helped

scrub. The puppy's coat had been tangled and even a little smelly, but soon he'd be all clean.

"I still don't know why you got to name him," said Hunter. "Shouldn't we all get a say, if he's our den project?"

"Yeah," said Sammy as he combed his fingers through Louie's tail.

Charles shrugged. "He'll always be Louie to me, but if you guys have any better ideas, let's hear them."

"Um," said Sammy.

"Spot," said Hunter.

Charles raised his eyebrows. Sammy laughed.

"Really? Is that the best you can do?" Charles asked.

"Because of his spots? What's wrong with that?" Hunter asked. "Okay, how about . . . Tiny? That would be kind of funny."

"Wait, wait! I know," said Sammy, who'd been

thinking so hard that his eyebrows were knit together. "Parker, because we found him at the park!"

Charles and Hunter both shook their heads. Sammy's face fell. "Yeah, I guess it's not so great," he said.

The boys were quiet for a while as they scrubbed. "I think that's enough soap," Charles said finally. "Let's rinse him off."

Sammy picked up the hose and held it over the big puppy as Charles and Hunter slid their hands through his fur, pushing the suds along as the cold water poured through the dog's coat. "Brrr!" said Charles. "Why are there still so many bubbles?" The soap was not going away—in fact, it seemed like the water was just making more lather. Louie was almost pure white now: the soapy bubbles covered all his black spots except for the ones on his face. The big puppy's patience seemed to be coming to an end. He raised his head and began to pull away from the boys.

Can this be over now? I'm not really having fun.

"Stand back!" Charles yelled. "I think he's about to shake."

Sure enough, Louie gave a mighty shake, and blobs of white lather flew all over the boys, the lawn, and the outdoor furniture.

"I guess I used a little too much baby shampoo," said Hunter, looking down at the half-empty bottle. "What do we do now?"

"We keep rinsing," Charles said. He dug into his pocket for one of the biscuits he had brought and coaxed the big pup back to his spot. "Come on, Louie," he said. "We'll be done soon." Charles's hands were almost numb from the cold water, but they had to finish what they'd started.

But Louie had other ideas. He charged toward the house, trailing clumps of suds.

I'm freezing! Let me in!

"No, Louie!" yelled Hunter as the wet pup pushed against the back door.

Charles ran to grab Louie's collar, but slipped in a pile of suds and fell to the grass.

"Louie, wait!" yelled Sammy. He dashed toward the soapy dog and pulled him away from the door.

Louie seemed to give in. With his head and tail hanging down, he let Sammy lead him back to the hose.

Charles smiled as the boys got back to work on rinsing the soapy dog. "Did you guys hear yourselves?" he asked. "I think it's decided. His name is Louie."

CHAPTER SEVEN

"Come in!" Mrs. Poole said when Charles and Tyler and Louie arrived at Liam's house the next day. "I've got snacks for everyone, including you, big guy." She knelt to give Louie a hug. "I got special permission for you to visit us," she told the big puppy. "I'm not supposed to have pets here, but I talked to my landlord and he made an exception, just for today."

Other people's houses are . . . different, Charles thought as he walked through the Pooles' living room. They looked different, with different furniture and different pictures on the walls. They smelled different—not better or worse necessarily, just different. They felt different, too. Liam's house was small but super cozy, and the kitchen smelled like cinnamon toast, which turned out to be what Liam's mom had just made for a snack. Charles felt comfortable there right away, and so did Louie.

Louie wagged his big flag of a tail and gave Liam's mom a big sloppy kiss.

I feel so welcome here!

Liam's mom giggled. "He doesn't seem so shy anymore," she said.

"We've been working on it," said Charles. "Lizzie even taught him a trick." He snapped his fingers to get Louie's attention. The big puppy sat up to look at Charles. "Louie, introduce yourself," Charles said.

Louie picked up one big paw and held it out in a "shake" gesture, for Liam's mom to grab. She laughed as they shook. "Nice to meet you, Louie," she said.

They all sat in the kitchen, the boys at high stools along the counter and Louie on the black-and-white linoleum floor. The boys munched on their cinnamon toast while Louie crunched a giant puppy biscuit.

"Your mother's article about Louie came out great," Liam's mom said to Charles. "She's a good reporter."

Charles nodded. "And the photographer took such a funny picture of Louie," he said. "I love the way his head is tilted."

"Have any tips been phoned in?" Liam asked. "You know, like if there were witnesses?"

Charles's mom had put a paragraph at the end

of her article asking people to call the newspaper if they had seen anything suspicious near Loon Lake that day. "Yes!" said Charles. "This one lady called to say she saw a white van going really fast up the road that day, and another person saw it, too. They both said it had a license plate from this state. They said they'd seen it around the area for a week or so before that day."

"Hmm," said Liam's mom. "Anything else?"

Charles shook his head. "That's about it, so far."

Tyler sighed. "So what can we do to find out more about where Louie came from?"

"Let's make a list," suggested Liam. He pulled out a pad and pencil. "Um," he said as he tapped the pencil on the pad.

"Usually, if we find a lost dog, we notify the police," said Charles. "And the local animal shelters, and vets."

"Vets! That's a great idea," said Liam's mom as Liam scribbled on the pad. "If the people were local, maybe they've taken Louie to a local vet. He's a pretty memorable puppy." She looked down at Louie. "Aren't you, big guy?" she asked.

Louie thumped his tail on the kitchen floor and looked hopefully at her hands.

Got any more of those biscuits?

Liam's mom pulled another big biscuit out of a paper bag and gave it to Louie. He thumped his tail again as he began to crunch and munch.

As soon as they finished their snacks, the boys began to make calls. Charles called Dr. Gibson, the vet they always went to with foster puppies who needed medical attention.

"Charles," she said. "Great to hear from you. Do you have a new puppy?"

"Yup," said Charles. "He's a big one, too. Lizzie says he's a Landseer."

Dr. Gibson laughed. "I bet he's sweet as pie, as well as being huge," she said. "I love Newfoundlands."

"Do you have any Landseer patients?" Charles asked. He explained about how they had found Louie.

Dr. Gibson gasped. "That's awful," she said. "Just when I think I've heard it all. What if nobody had noticed that crate in the parking lot?"

Charles felt his stomach flip over. He hadn't really thought about that. It sure was lucky that Liam's mom had run by when she had.

"Anyway," said Dr. Gibson, "I only have one Landseer as a patient, and he's eight years old. Not a puppy. But I'll put the word out to other vets in the area, and we'll see what we can find out."

Charles thanked her and hung up. Next, they called Ms. Dobbins at Caring Paws, who had already seen his mom's article in the newspaper. "I'm on the case," she said. "I hope we find those people. They need to understand how wrong it was to do what they did."

Finally, Charles called the local police. He talked to Tim Oliver, who ran the K-9 program, which trained dogs to work with police partners. Charles had met Tim when his family fostered Champ, a brave and beautiful German shepherd. "We'll keep an eye out for that white van," Chief promised. "But if you really want to do some detective work, I'd suggest you go back to that park and look for clues. Interview every neighbor up and down the street in case they saw something suspicious. You might be surprised what you can find out."

All the boys liked the idea of going to the park.

"We'll be like real detectives," said Tyler. "I'll bring my magnifying glass."

"I'll bring a notebook," said Liam.

"And I'll bring Louie," said Charles. "Who knows? Maybe that big puppy nose of his will sniff out some clues."

CHAPTER EIGHT

Things were still pretty quiet when Charles's dad took the boys down to Loon Lake Park after school the next day. "Opening day is this weekend," said Charles, pointing to a sign at the park's welcome booth. "Free ice cream and free canoe rentals all day," he read. "Cool! We should have another picnic down here on Saturday."

"Hunter and me always have a contest to see which of us goes swimming first every spring," said Tyler. "Last year he won. He jumped in on April Fools' Day! This year I'm going to win."

"I don't know," said Liam. "That water still looks pretty cold to me." He rubbed his arms. "Brrr."

"Louie doesn't seem to mind," said Charles. "Look at him go."

Louie had pulled the leash out of Charles's hand, dashed right past the welcome booth, and charged into the shallow water near the canoe racks, chasing some geese who had been floating on the choppy, gray waves. Now he swam in big circles, happily splashing away as the geese honked and flapped their wings at him.

"Lizzie was right about his breed," said Dad. "He is an amazing swimmer!"

"Come on, Louie," said Charles. "Leave the geese alone, now." He whistled and waved. "Louie!"

Finally, the dog turned and swam back toward shore with powerful, sure strokes. When he emerged from the water, he raced up and down the beach, stopped to shake off, then lay down and rolled happily in the sand. Charles groaned. "So much for his bath," he said. "Come on, Louie, we have to look for clues." He went over and clipped the big dog's leash onto his collar. "Ready?"

Louie grinned a doggy grin up at him and shook off again, spraying all the boys with water and gritty sand.

I'm always ready for an adventure!

"Ugh!" said Tyler.

Liam just laughed.

"Louie," groaned Charles, wiping at his pants.

"You were the one who wanted to foster a big sloppy dog again," his dad reminded him with a smile.

"I know, I know," said Charles. "And he's worth it." He tousled Louie's wet ears. "Aren't you, big guy?"

"Let's go look for clues." Tyler pulled a huge magnifying glass out of his pocket and put it up to his face. Charles and Liam laughed at the giant eye staring back at them.

"Maybe we should head back to the upper parking lot, where we first found Louie," Dad suggested. "I don't see any clues down here."

Louie led the way as they hiked across the little bridge and up the path through the woods. As they came out into the parking lot, he stopped still and stared.

"What is it, Louie?" Charles asked. He peered down to the end of the parking lot. A man and a woman stood near the spot where Louie's crate had been.

Louie leaned against Charles's knee. Then he took a few paces forward and tugged at the leash, staring at the people. Then he slunk back again to Charles.

"Louie?" Charles asked. "What's the matter?"

Then the woman turned around and spotted

them. "Harley!" she shouted. She knelt and opened her arms.

The man turned, too. "What?" he said. "It's really him! Come here, boy!"

Louie didn't seem to know what to do. He looked up at Charles.

They're my people. But—I'm scared. And confused.

Charles's dad strode toward the couple. "Hello," he said. "I'm Paul Peterson. And you are?"

"We are that dog's owners," said the man, pointing to Louie. "I'm Steven, and this is Sarah."

"You *were* his owners," Dad corrected. "If I'm not wrong, you abandoned him here." He looked back at Charles and Louie.

"We didn't mean to," blurted Sarah. She looked as if she'd been crying. "I mean, we did leave him here, but then we realized that it was the wrong way to do it. We came back—but he was already gone."

"We just couldn't keep him," said Steven. "We lost our lease at our apartment just after I lost my job. We've basically been living out of our van. We were—well, we were staying here in the park, even though it's not open yet."

"It's been so stressful," said Sarah. "Harley picked up on it. He'd try to run away or hide under the van every time we had an argument. We thought he'd be better off in a real home. We were going to call the animal shelter to let them know where we'd left him—but then he wasn't here anymore. We didn't know what to do."

"And now you're back at the scene of the crime!" announced Tyler, looking at them through his magnifying glass. "Classic. That's what all the criminals do. They can't stay away."

"We're not criminals!" said Sarah.

"We came back because we thought maybe he'd escaped from the crate and was looking for us," said Steven. "We wanted to make sure he was okay."

Louie was still leaning against Charles's leg. Charles scratched the top of the big puppy's head. "He didn't escape," he said. "We rescued him. My family is fostering him until we can find him a good home."

Sarah's eyes brimmed with tears. "We miss you so much, Harley," she said. She held out her hand. Finally, Louie ran to her. She buried her face in his fur. Steven knelt down to hug the dog, too.

Charles looked at his dad. Now what? Did they have to give Louie back to the people who had abandoned him?

CHAPTER NINE

On Saturday, opening day at Loon Lake Park, Charles and his family—and the whole Cub Scout den and their families—got together for another picnic. Charles and his dad told everyone what had happened with Sarah and Steven.

"I still can't forgive them," said Lizzie for the fortieth time since she'd heard about it. "How could they leave a dog alone like that?"

"They just weren't thinking straight," said Dad. "Steven and Sarah are going through a very rough time right now. They were really sad about having to give up their dog—but now they understand that there are better ways to do that.

They're hoping to get another dog once they are back on their feet, and I'm sure they would never make the same mistake again."

"Anyway, Louie is safe with us now," said Charles. "After we explained about how we foster dogs, Sarah and Steven were happy to know that we're going to find him a good home. They even said it's okay to keep calling him Louie if we can't get used to Harley. Probably whoever adopts him will change his name, anyway." He passed his sister a Popsicle he had just gotten from the ice cream stand. "Come on, forget about all that. Let's have some fun—like Louie!"

He pointed to the beach, where Louie and Buddy were wading in the shallow water, splashing through the tiny waves as they chased the ball Mom was tossing for them. Charles was so glad that dogs were allowed at Loon Lake.

"I have to give you guys credit," said Lizzie. "I think Louie's ready for a new home, with all the work you've done with him. Your den project is a success." She held up a hand.

Charles returned Lizzie's high five. "It's easy when you're working with a dog like Louie. He's such a good boy."

"A real sweetheart," agreed his dad.

There were other families at the lake that day, too, and other dogs—Charles spotted a husky and a Pomeranian, two breeds he knew from fostering experience. People were throwing Frisbees and grilling hot dogs. Kids were racing around the playground, swinging on the swings and sliding down the slide. The kayaks and canoes were off their racks and floating in the water. Each one was tethered by a rope to the long dock, ready for boaters to take out. Loon Lake Park was all set for summer—but it wasn't exactly summer yet.

The water was still cold. So far there were no kids jumping off the dock, or showing off their special dives, or floating on blow-up rafts.

Still, Tyler and Hunter had put on their swim trunks and raced down to the water. Seconds later, they raced back to the picnic tables. "It's freezing!" said Tyler.

"So cold!" said Hunter. "I could only put one toe in. I don't know how Louie and Buddy can take it." He reached for his sweatshirt and pants and pulled his clothes on over his suit.

"I told you it was too early for swimming." Mrs. Pagano laughed. "It won't be warm enough for a few weeks."

"Can we go out in a canoe?" Tyler asked.

Their parents looked at each other, then their mom nodded. "Go pick one out, and we'll take it for a paddle after we eat."

"Can we go, too?" Liam asked his mom.

"Sure," said Mrs. Poole. "Or maybe we'll take one of those double kayaks."

Soon all the scouts were down by the dock, looking over the boats.

"I learned how to steer a canoe when I was at camp last summer," said Sammy. "The steerer sits in the back. You use the paddle in a special way to make the canoe go to the left or right."

"Stern," said Liam.

"What?" asked Sammy.

"The back is called the stern," Liam said. "And left and right are port and starboard." He grinned. "I went to camp, too. But I never got that good at steering. I like to sit up front—in the bow—and paddle."

"Maybe we should do a canoe trip someday," said Charles. "We could bring all our camping stuff and go up a river, like Lewis and Clark." He had once done a project on the explorers, and he'd never forgotten their amazing adventures.

Liam pointed to a sleek red kayak with two seats. "I want to learn how to paddle one of those," he said. "I bet you can go really fast."

Hunter and Tyler had walked down to the end of the dock and climbed into one of the big green canoes.

"Hey," said Charles. "You're not supposed to go out in those without a life jacket on."

"We're not going anywhere," said Tyler. "We don't even have paddles. We're just checking it out. Come on in! It's cool."

Liam and Sammy got into the canoe, stepping in carefully to keep it from tipping. Charles stood on the dock, not so sure he wanted to get in. The canoe was already beginning to look a little low in the water with four boys in it.

Tyler started to shift his weight from side to side, and the canoe tilted wildly. "Woo-hoo!" cried Tyler.

"Cut it out!" said Sammy.

"Hey, stop it," said Liam, grabbing on to the sides of the canoe.

Hunter started throwing his weight in the opposite direction. Water swished up around the canoe.

"Boys!" Charles heard Hunter and Tyler's mom shout as she ran down from the picnic tables. "Get out of that boat right now."

At that moment, the canoe flipped over, and all four boys fell into the water with a huge splash.

CHAPTER TEN

Hunter and Tyler bobbed right up with big grins on their faces. "I won!" said Hunter.

"No, I did!" said Tyler.

Sammy splashed his way toward the dock, flipping his hair out of his eyes. "Phew, that's cold!" he said as he hauled himself out.

"Where's Liam?" asked Mrs. Pagano. "Liam!"

Just then, Charles saw Liam's head break the surface of the water. "Can't swim!" he gasped, before he sank down again.

Charles didn't even stop to think. He jumped off the dock toward Liam. He knew that the water was deep only at the very end of the dock—if he could pull Liam in just a few feet, the water wouldn't be over his head.

The water was so cold it took Charles's breath away. But there was no time to get used to it. He swam as hard as he could toward Liam.

As he got closer, Liam popped out of the water again, yelling and flailing his arms. "Help!" he said. "Can't swim!"

Charles wasn't sure what to do. How could he grab Liam without getting bashed?

He heard a big splash behind him. A moment later, Louie passed him, swimming with powerful strokes straight for Liam. The dog ignored the flailing arms and grabbed Liam's shirt in his jaws. Then he powered back toward shore, towing the boy along until Liam's feet touched the bottom.

It all happened in a few seconds. By now, all the

adults were standing at the shore. Liam's mother ran to pick him up out of the shallows as he waded onto the sand. "Oh, sweetie," she said as she held him close. Charles, wading in behind Liam, saw tears streaming down her face. "Are you okay?"

He coughed. "I'm fine," he said.

Sammy's mom ran to Sammy with a towel and wrapped him up in it.

"What were you thinking?" the twins' father asked them. "I've told you never to get into a boat without life jackets on."

Hunter hung his head. "Sorry," he said. "We were just fooling around."

"Sorry, Liam," said Tyler. "I didn't know you couldn't swim."

"Even if he could," said their mom, "that's not the point. No more boats for you two. Not today, maybe not all summer." She shook her head. "I'm very disappointed in you boys." Then she knelt down and opened her arms. "And I'm also very glad you're safe," she said. The twins ran to her for a hug, and their father joined in, too.

Charles's mom hugged him and rubbed her hands up and down his arms. "You must be freezing," she said. "Let's go get you a towel."

"That was some brave thing you did there, chief," said Charles's dad.

Charles ducked his head. "I didn't do anything," he said. "Louie's the one who saved Liam."

"Louie!" Liam wasn't coughing anymore. His voice was loud and clear. They all turned to see Louie rolling on the grass, his feet dancing in the air. The big pup jumped up and shook himself off, then stood wagging his tail, a big doggy grin on his face.

That's my name—or at least I guess it is now!

"Louie!" all the boys yelled as they raced over to hug him.

Louie wasn't shy now. This time, he just stood and wagged and grinned while the boys climbed all over him.

"You're a hero, Louie," said Tyler.

"Definitely not a wimp," said Hunter.

Charles laughed. Finally, the twins had found something they agreed on. "You did it," he said to the big puppy as he kissed Louie's nose.

"Louie, Louie, Louie!" chanted Sammy.

Liam just threw his arms around Louie's neck and pressed his face into the big dog's wet fur.

"Well, I guess this settles it," said Mrs. Poole as they all walked back to the picnic tables. "I've been talking to my landlord about buying the house we're renting, and he's agreed. Do you know what that means, Liam?" She smiled down at him.

He shook his head. "That we won't have to move again anytime soon?" he asked.

"Well, yes," said his mom. "But something else, too. If we own our house instead of renting it, we can have a dog if we want."

Liam stared at her. "A dog?" he asked.

"Well, not just any dog," said Mrs. Poole. "I've been thinking maybe we should adopt Louie—and then what happened today made me sure that we should."

All the boys cheered. "Louie, Louie, Louie!" chanted Tyler and Hunter.

Charles grinned. He knew Louie would be really happy living with Liam and his mom. "And he can still be our Cub Scout project, too," he said. "If you ever want help with training or taking care of him, I mean. We all love Louie."

"Agreed," said Mrs. Pagano. "This is one dog I will be honored to allow in my house—anytime."

"We'd love to have him, too," said Sammy's dad. "The big lug is welcome over at our place."

"And ours, of course," said Charles's mom.

All five boys ran over to hug Louie. "Welcome to the den," said Charles. Louie wagged his tail and wriggled all over with happiness as he tried to lick every face at once. The big puppy had found not just one perfect home, but four!

PUPPY TIPS

I'm sure most of my readers know that it is never okay to abandon a dog or puppy—or any pet!—the way Louie was abandoned. There are times when people are unable to keep a pet they love. This can happen for many reasons: moving, allergies, a pet who is just not fitting in with the family. In these cases, it's always best to take the pet to a local animal shelter or foster care family, where it will be cared for until a new home can be found. It was sad to write about an abandoned puppy, but these things do happen. In fact, this story was inspired by something I heard about on the news!

Dear Reader,

Would you like to make cinnamon toast like Liam's mother did? It's one of my favorite treats. Here's the recipe: Toast some bread (raisin bread is especially good!) and spread butter on it. Then sprinkle on some sugar and some cinnamon and let it melt into the butter as you spread it around. Yum!

Be sure to give your dog a treat, too.

Yours from the Puppy Place,

Ellen Miles

"Hi, Misha, hi!" Lizzie Peterson squatted down to pet the wriggly, panting husky. The dog hardly knew her, but like all dogs he was always happy to see a friendly person. She ruffled the thick white fur around Misha's neck and gazed into his blue eyes. "How's my handsome boy?" she said.

He grinned a doggie grin at her and wriggled some more, wagging his fluffy tail hard. Lizzie could tell that he was about to jump on her, so she distracted him by standing up. "Sit," she told him, as she gave a hand signal. Misha sat. Now his tail swept the floor as he wagged, still grinning up at her.

Lizzie laughed. The best thing about her job was the happy dogs. Lizzie, her best friend, and two other girls had a dog-walking business, taking care of dogs for people who wanted their pets to have a little extra attention and exercise. Lizzie loved to help with training, too; she was the one who had taught Misha how to sit, and she was working on the jumping-up issue.

Every day—at least, every school day, her clients' dogs waited patiently for her to arrive. And when she did, every single dog behaved as if she was the best thing that had happened all day. She was greeted with wags and wriggles, kisses and excited barks. It always felt great.

"It's so easy to make you guys happy," Lizzie told Misha, as she looked for his leash. "A few pats, maybe a treat, and you've made a new bestie. Now, where do they keep your stuff?"

Misha was not one of Lizzie's regular charges. Normally, he was on Daphne's route. Lizzie was covering for Daphne, who wanted her afternoons off because her aunt was visiting from Colorado. "Please?" Daphne had asked. "She's my favorite aunt and I never get to see her. She wants to take me shopping and to the movies and stuff."

Lizzie didn't mind. She liked meeting new dogs, and visiting with ones she had met before, like Misha. She just wished Daphne kept better notes on the dogs she walked. Lizzie checked the index card she had pulled out of her pocket. *Misha*, it said. *Husky, six years old. Pulls on leash. Very strong. Likes to chase squirrels.* All of that was helpful, but pretty predictable if you knew anything about huskies. Lizzie also really needed to know what commands Misha knew, whether he was allowed to eat just any dog treats or if he was allergic to wheat or anything else, and . . . "And where is your leash?" she asked Misha.

Misha pranced to a cabinet near the front door and put a paw on it. Lizzie laughed again. "It's in there?" she asked. "Are you sure?"

Misha took a few steps back, sat down, and woo-wooed, throwing his head back to let out a few soft, short howls. Lizzie loved the woo-woo that huskies did instead of barking. Once she'd even met someone who had taught her husky how to say "I love you," in howls. It sounded more like "Wyyy wuuuuuvvvv wooooooohhh!," and it was hilarious.

Lizzie pulled the cabinet door open. "Yes!" she said. There it was, a handsome red-leather leash hanging on a hook. "Good boy. You *do* know where your leash is, don't you?" She took the leash out and snapped it onto Misha's collar. "Great, now we can go." Lizzie knew she had everything else she might need in her backpack: dog treats (she always carried wheat-free ones just in case), a bottle of water, poop bags, and even a doggie emergency kit, with bandages and other supplies. She had gotten that when she took a course on canine first aid at the community center. There, Lizzie had learned to bandage paws, clean cuts, and even do doggy CPR, helping an unconscious dog with his breathing. So far she had not had to use anything she'd learned, except once when her own puppy, Buddy, cut his foot on a piece of glass.

Poor little Buddy. As Lizzie walked Misha down the street, she pictured her sweet brown puppy looking up at her with the saddest eyes as he held out his bleeding paw. She smiled as she remembered how he'd licked her cheek as thanks after she was done cleaning and bandaging the cut.

Buddy had first come to the Petersons' as a foster puppy. They had fostered many puppies before and after Buddy, keeping each one just long enough to find it the perfect home—but Buddy was the only one who came to stay. The whole family—Lizzie, her parents, and her two younger brothers, Charles and the Bean—had fallen madly in love with the adorable mixed-breed pup. There was no question that Buddy was their favorite puppy ever.

"But I do like you, too, Misha," Lizzie told the husky. He was prancing around now, still wearing that silly grin. She knew he was more than ready for his walk. "Let's go then," she said, as they headed out the back door together.

"Misha, Misha!" Lizzie heard the sound of girls' voices. Even before she had come around the corner of the house, they had spotted the dog. Misha heard the voices, too. He strained at his leash, tugging Lizzie toward the sidewalk.

He dragged her straight for two little girls—older than the Bean but younger than Charles—*Maybe about five years old?* Lizzie guessed. They must have been playing in the yard next door, where Lizzie spotted a swing set.

Before she could even think of the best way to slow him down, Misha tugged her right up to the girls. They laughed and thumped him and petted him and stroked his long, fluffy tail. "Misha, Misha," they repeated.

Then one of them, with long, shiny dark hair and deep dark eyes to match, stopped to stare at Lizzie. "Who are you?" she asked.

Lizzie smiled. "I'm Lizzie. I'm taking over for Daphne this week."

"Daphne, Daphne!" they yelled.

"We know Daphne," said the other girl, who was wiry and strong looking, with red hair and freckles. "We go with her on her walks. Can we come with you? I'm Jeannette and that's Gloria."

"If your moms say yes, sure!" said Lizzie. The girls were adorable. "Where do you live?"

"Right there," said Gloria, pointing to the big white house next door to Misha's. "And we only have one mom."

"Oh," said Lizzie. "Okay, well let's ask her." She was surprised that they were sisters. They did not look alike.

They each grabbed one of Lizzie's hands and pulled her up the front walk. "Mommy, Mommy," they yelled.

Their mom came to the door. *She doesn't look a thing like either girl*, Lizzie thought. She had curly light blonde hair, almost white.

"Hi," Lizzie said. "I'm Lizzie Peterson. I'm the

president of the dog-walking business your neighbor Daphne works for."

The woman raised her eyebrows. "Funny, somehow I always thought Daphne was the president," she said.

Lizzie smiled. "Well, we're all kind of the president," she said. "Anyway, is it okay if your girls walk with me? I'm just going around the block, and I'm used to watching little kids."

"How about if I come along?" She stuck out her hand. "I'm Allie. Allie Bauer."

"Great," said Lizzie. "Next stop is to pick up Ruby."

Allie shook her head. "Nope, next stop is Winnie."

Lizzie checked the sheet Daphne had given her, with all her clients' names and addresses. "I don't see a Winnie," she said.

"Oh, Daphne doesn't walk her," said Allie. "We all just love to visit her. Right, girls?"

"Winnie, Winnie!" yelled the girls.

Allie and Lizzie laughed. "They sure do love that puppy," Allie said.

Then Lizzie heard noises. A bark, a whimper, a whine. The puppy was not far off, and she must have heard the sisters calling her name. "Let's go," said Lizzie.

ABOUT THE AUTHOR

Ellen Miles loves dogs, which is why she has a great time writing the Puppy Place books. And guess what? She loves cats, too! (In fact, her very first pet was a beautiful tortoiseshell cat named Jenny.) That's why she came up with the Kitty Corner series. Ellen lives in Vermont and loves to be outdoors with her dog, Zipper, every day, walking, biking, skiing, or swimming, depending on the season. She also loves to read, cook, explore her beautiful state, play with dogs, and hang out with friends and family.

Visit Ellen at www.ellenmiles.net.